The Extraordinarily Ordinary Life of Cassandra Jones

Walker Wildcats Year 1: Age 10

Episode 1: The New Girl

The Extraordinarily Ordinary Life of Cassandra Jones
Walker Wildcats Year 1

Episode 1: The New Girl
Episode 2: Club Girls
Episode 3: Road Trip
Episode 4: Fever Pitch
Episode 5: Miss Popular
Episode 6: Reaching Higher

Tamara Hart Heiner

Also by Tamara Hart Heiner:
Perilous (WiDo Publishing 2010)
Altercation (WiDo Publishing 2012)
Deliverer (Tamark Publishing 2014)

Inevitable (Tamark Publishing 2013)

Tornado Warning (Dancing Lemur Press 2014)

Print Edition, License Notes:

TABLE OF CONTENTS

CHAPTER ONE

New School

The van door slid shut behind Cassandra Jones as her brother climbed out, and still she stood in front of the new school, staring up at it. Her heart thumped out a staccato rhythm at double time. *Duh-dum, duh-dum, duh-dum.* She knew where her classroom was; her mom had shown her when they visited the school a few days ago. No, that wasn't the problem.

The problem was, she didn't know anyone. Last year had been the best one ever at North Ridge Elementary. She spent every spare moment with her best friend, Tammy. Her mind flashed on those images now, eating lunch together, running on the playground, trying to see who could go the highest on the swing set at Tammy's house.

They'd left Texas right after the last day of school. As in, Cassandra walked out the school doors, talking with Tammy, and saw her mom's van waiting in the pick up line. The whole family was already inside, the vehicle packed to the rafters with everything the moving truck hadn't taken.

And in that moment, the gravity of the situation hit Cassandra like a grand piano. She thrust her arms around Tammy and sobbed into her shoulder.

"Cassie. Cassie!"

Her mom's voice behind her made Cassandra zone back into reality. She blinked back moisture and turned to the open window and the van that hadn't moved.

"Cassandra, I'm holding up the line," her mom said, weary lines etched around her eyes. Still, she pursed her lips together, and Cassandra knew her mother wasn't unsympathetic to her plight. "You've got to go inside, Cassie. You're going to be fine."

Cassandra nodded and forced her feet to step forward. Her younger brother and sister were already gone, fearless in the face of the unknown. They just didn't know enough to be scared. Cassie did. She was a fifth grader now, and she knew how mean kids could be. She'd had a good group of friends in Texas, solid protection. She had nothing here.

Being late wasn't the first impression she wanted to make, either. She quickened her pace and ducked into the classroom, depositing her lunch box next to the others lined up against the wall. She found the desk Ms. Dawson had showed her last week and settled into it. Cassandra kept her eyes down while surveying her new classmates out of the corner of her eye. A boy with brown hair and glasses chatted with another boy, and a girl with short, reddish-blond hair showed off her new folders to a larger brunette. A few glanced her way, but most paid her no mind.

Cassie felt the breath slide out of her, and some of the tension worked its way out of her shoulders. This couldn't be that bad, then. Nobody laughed at her or pointed her out as the new girl.

The eight o'clock bell rang, and the teacher started the class. She called roll. Cassandra tried to pay attention to the names, but they passed by in a blur. She remembered to call out "Here" when Ms. Dawson read, "Cassandra Jones."

"Sometimes I go by Cassie." The sentence was at the tip of her tongue, but she delayed too long and was too timid, and Ms. Dawson had already moved on.

Ms. Dawson gave out orders to organize their school supplies before copying down the sentences on the board. Copying sentences. This was familiar and easy, if not boring. The class worked in silence, and Cassie didn't have to worry about whether anyone would speak to her.

"All right, it's time for morning recess," the teacher said, and Cassie's traitorous heart started to gallop again. Would anyone play with her? Would she be left alone at the sidewalk?

The New Girl

"Let's line up alphabetically." Ms. Dawson read out their names, and each child stood in turn and lined up at the door. "Matthew Higgins. Riley Isabel. Cassandra Jones."

Cassandra stood, smoothing down the skirt of her first-day-of-school dress. She never wore dresses except Sundays and the first day of school. In fact, until recently she had considered herself a tomboy, happier up in a tree than with a doll. But she'd felt a secret thrill of pleasure when her mother removed the curlers this morning and Cassandra caught a glimpse of her reflection, red pleated dress and full curls tumbling down her back. She looked pretty.

The girl with the short strawberry-blond hair was in front of her. She cast a glance back at Cassie and faced the front again. Cassie wanted to say hi, but the thought of speaking out loud when no one had called on her made her throat go dry. Instead she planned what she would say the next time the girl turned around.

They marched down the hall in a semi-straight line, some kids dragging their feet or walking slightly out of sync with the rest. As soon as they burst through the back doors to the play yard, however, the line dissolved. Children filtered out like ants from a scattered anthill. It was a large play yard, with a soccer field on one side, swings, tether balls, monkey bars, and a metal dome climber in the middle, and trees on the other side.

"Wow," Cassie said, speaking in spite of herself. "It's so big."

"There's more on the other side," Matthew said,

still standing close to her. "This is the upper grades playground." He looked at her and then turned away, his cheeks coloring. He dashed off the sidewalk and joined the other kids.

Cassie smiled. She wasn't an outsider, then. Someone had spoken to her.

She didn't join in with the other girls. She didn't know them well enough. Instead Cassie went to the swings. She pumped her legs and went as high as she could. Up here, with the wind streaking through her hair and around her ears, no one else existed. It didn't really matter if she knew anyone or had friends.

Ms. Dawson blew her whistle, and kids withdrew from different areas of the play yard, regrouping as if sucked in by a magnet. "Line up in order!" she shouted.

Cassie looked around for the short-haired girl. She waited until the other girl had stepped into line, and then Cassie got in behind her. "Hi," she said, gathering up her courage.

The girl didn't even turn around. Maybe she hadn't heard.

They cleaned up after recess and did some book work before going to lunch. Kids with lunch boxes lined up on one side, and those buying lunch lined up on the other. Cassie noted with relief that meant she wouldn't have to be next to the short-haired girl.

She didn't have the chance to wonder who would sit by her, either. They filed into the cafeteria and sat down at their table in the same order they'd been in line. Cassie opened up her blue lunch box, wondering if her mom had remembered that she didn't like peanut butter and jelly sandwiches.

Someone tapped her on the shoulder. "Cassandra?"

She looked up, trying to hide her surprise.

The brunette from her class stood there. She brushed her shoulder-length hair back, balancing her lunch tray on her hip. "Want to come and eat lunch with me?"

Cassie looked toward the table by the windows where she pointed, with another teacher and several other kids. "Am I allowed to do that?"

The brunette smiled, showing colorful elastic bands around the braces on her teeth. "Yep."

"Sure." Cassie packed her lunch back up and followed the other girl. She tried to contain her joy, but she felt as if she'd won a prize. Someone she didn't know wanted to eat lunch with her.

"I'm Danelle," the girl said as they sat down with the other students.

"And I'm Ms. Buckley," the teacher said. She had short blond hair and tiny wrinkles around her eyes. She smiled at Danelle. "I'm the school counselor."

"Hi," Cassie said, unwrapping her peanut butter and jelly sandwich. Great. "I'm Cassandra. You can call me Cassie."

The other kids introduced themselves, and Cassie realized half of them were new, also. Cassie nodded at them and put her sandwich aside for the other food offerings in her box. Grapes, chips, thermos of milk.

"You don't like your sandwich?" Danelle asked.

Cassie shook her head. "Not really."

"Here, trade with me." Not even asking, Danelle

swapped out Cassie's sandwich for her chicken fingers. "It's my favorite."

"Thanks," Cassie said, staring in wonder at her. What would it be like to have that kind of confidence? To be so sure of herself and others around her?

"So where did you move from?" Danelle asked, biting into the soft white bread and speaking around the food.

"Texas," Cassie said, warming to the subject. "I loved it there. I miss all my friends. But my dad, he got a job transfer. So now we're here."

"In Arkansas," Danelle said, taking a swallow of milk.

Cassie nodded, feeling her smile slip a bit. "Yeah."

"What do you think of it so far?" Ms. Buckley

asked.

She hesitated in her response. She hated it here, and they'd only lived here three months. She hated the small apartment that passed for their house, hated that all her friends were still in Texas, hated the snakes and spiders she spotted anytime she walked outside.

But she knew she couldn't say that. "The people are nice," she said. She tacked a big smile on to the end of the sentence, hoping Ms. Buckley would buy it.

"That's right," Danelle said, nodding. "The nicest people ever here."

⚬⟞⟝⟞⚬

Turned out that Danelle's last name was Pierce, and she was two people behind Cassie at line up.

"Hi," she said to Cassie when they lined up for

afternoon recess.

"Hi," Cassie said back, grinning. They met up again outside.

"Do you like to swing?" Danelle asked.

"My most favorite thing!" Cassie replied. They raced to the swings, each girl pushing harder to make hers go the highest.

When Ms. Dawson blew her whistle, Danelle jumped off without even stopping her swing. "Come on, Cassandra!"

Cassie hesitated. Tammy had told her horror stories about people jumping off of swings and cracking their heads open. She'd always been too afraid to try.

"Silly goose!" Danelle said. "We have to line up!"

Cassie tucked her legs under her before thinking

maybe that wasn't such a good idea. Instead she straightened them, took a deep breath, and jumped off. The momentum flung her forward, and her legs struggled to keep up. She stumbled through the grass until Danelle grabbed her arm, laughing.

"I can tell you haven't done that before," she said.

"Yeah," Cassie agreed.

"You'll have plenty of chances to practice." She raced on ahead, and Cassie followed, breathless.

⁙

Today, and today only, Cassie's mom waited for them in the car line. Tomorrow they would all ride the bus to the apartment in Fayetteville. The idea rather excited her. She'd never been on a bus before except for field trips.

She found her brother and sister, Scott and Emily,

waiting outside with the mobs of students. "How was school?" she asked them.

"Great," Emily said, and she launched into a lengthy description of the classroom rules and what activities they had done. Cassie tuned her out. She hadn't really wanted a play-by-play.

"Scott?" she asked.

"Boring," he replied.

"You're in first grade!" Cassie said. "How can it be boring?"

He shrugged.

Cassie waited for someone to ask her, but no one did. So she stated, "Well, my day was great. I've already made a new best friend." She waited for a reaction, but Emily and Scott just stared at her. Cassie let out a dramatic sigh. "Don't you get it? If you don't have a best friend, you don't have anyone to hang out with. No one to tell your secrets to. No one to celebrate with you when you do great. No one to play with at recess. Having a best friend is the most important part of school!"

Emily's face lit up, and Cassie knew she'd caught on. "Yeah! I made a best friend."

"Not me," Scott grumbled. "I didn't make any friends."

"Bye, Emily!" someone called. All three of them swiveled to view a girl with long blond hair and big blue glasses waving as she got into a car.

"Bye!" Emily called back, waving emphatically. "See you tomorrow!"

"That your new best friend?" Cassie asked.

"No. I can't remember her name. My new best

friend is Alyssa. She sits by me."

"Ah," Cassie said. "My best friend is. . . ." Her words trailed off as she took stock of the waiting area. Only about five kids still lingered around the curb, but there were no more cars in line. "Where's Mom?"

A teacher came out of the school, a slight frown crinkling her forehead. "All right, everyone inside. We'll start calling parents in a few minutes."

"Were we supposed to ride the bus?" Emily said, her brown eyes wide and fearful. "Maybe Mom's at home waiting for us!"

"No, we weren't!" Cassie snapped, her sudden worry making her cross. Her head pounded with an oncoming headache. Mom wouldn't forget them, would she? She never had before. At their old school, they would walk several blocks and meet up with the car. Had she expected them to walk? Cassie shook her head. Couldn't be. She wouldn't even know which direction to go.

They trooped into the hallway between the entrance and the office. The other kids sat down on their backpacks or rested their heads on them, all looking tired and defeated.

"Where's your mom?" Scott asked a little boy.

He gave a shrug. "She'll be here. She's always late."

"Late," Scott echoed, as if tasting the word.

Cassie squeezed her fists together and stared out the window, willing the blue van to appear. Any moment now, her mom would come into view, apologizing for whatever had kept her from being here on time.

A yellow car slid against the curb, and the little boy jumped up and ran outside.

The teacher came into view again. "Okay, let's start calling parents." She pointed at Cassie. "We'll start with you."

Cassie stared at the teacher, her mouth suddenly going dry. She'd just remembered something. She didn't know their new phone number.

CHAPTER TWO

Misunderstandings

Cassie followed the teacher into the office, squeezing her hands together as she went. The woman picked up the phone and handed it to Cassie. "Um, it's just," Cassie whispered.

"What?" The woman leaned closer. "I couldn't hear you."

"I don't know my phone number," she whispered.

The teacher sighed and put the phone down. She went behind the desk and opened up a filing cabinet. "What's your last name?"

"Jones."

She thumbed through and stopped on one. "First name?"

"Cassandra."

The thumbing resumed until she found what she wanted. She pulled it from the cabinet and picked up the phone. "Is this a cell phone or a landline?" she asked, punching the numbers into the phone.

"Landline," Cassie answered.

The woman handed the phone to Cassie. She pressed it to her ear, listening to the monotone ring.

Then it stopped, and her mother's voice on the machine picked up.

"You've reached the Jones's. Leave us a message, and we'll get back to you as soon as we can!"

She hung up before the beep and shook her head. "No answer."

"Well, she must be on her way here." The teacher didn't look too pleased. She ushered Cassie back into the hallway and disappeared into the office with another student.

"Did you reach Mom?" Emily asked, chewing on her fingernails.

Cassie looked down at her own nails. She'd broken the chewing habit just this summer, but she had the urge to start up again. "No. She's probably almost here."

The words were barely out of her mouth when the blue van pulled into the parking lot, coming to a hasty stop at the curb in front of the doors. Emily and Scott bolted from the hallway. Cassie followed behind, her relief morphing into anger. First day of school. How could she do that to them?

She climbed into the front seat and settled her backpack on the floor as Emily blabbed away about what a great first day it had been. Putting on her seatbelt, Cassie interrupted. "What happened? Was there a car accident? An emergency."

Her mother shot her a weary look. "No, Cassandra. No emergency. I'm very sorry I'm late."

And that was it? No further explanation? Cassie wasn't ready to let it go. "First day of school, Mom. And you weren't there." She didn't feel like talking about the way the teacher had looked at them, the way it felt to be forgotten with the other kids who expected to be forgotten. "Why weren't you there?"

Her mom pressed her lips together. "We live farther away than I thought. It won't happen again. From now on, you're on the bus."

Cassie leaned her head back and released a sigh. That was something, at least.

"What about you?" her mom said, attempting conversation. "How was school?"

Cassie shrugged. "Fine. It was fine."

They pulled away from the curb, but didn't head the direction Cassie expected. "Where are we going?" she asked.

"To the new house." Her mom gave her a smile. "We should have everything ready to move in this weekend."

"Really?" Cassie gasped.

"Yay!" Emily cheered in the back. Even Scott looked excited, and nothing excited him. Anette didn't look up from her dolls. She probably didn't care.

They took back roads out to the countryside. No wonder her mom hadn't been on time. Cassie looked at the plantation-style house, more anxious than ever to move into it. The two-bedroom apartment they were staying in was way too crowded for the six of them. She wanted her space back.

Mr. Jones's small green sports car was already parked in the driveway, a large white moving van in the circle drive. He greeted Mrs. Jones with a kiss, and then the kids exploded out of the van, heading for the house.

"Grab a box," he shouted, gesturing to the moving truck. "Don't go in empty-handed."

"But we don't know where things go," Cassie said.

"Just put it inside somewhere."

They trudged back and Cassie picked up a smaller box labeled "kitchen." Okay, so maybe she could figure out where this one went. She pushed open the front door, walking through the tiled entryway and to the kitchen. Both tables had already been set up. She put the box on the dining room table and headed for the bedroom she shared with Emily.

She sighed in contentment. It wasn't a big room, but it would just be the two of them, instead of all four like it was now. The bunk bed was already set up. Cassie pulled open the accordion doors that shielded the closet. There was a bookshelf for her books. Suddenly she wanted to get all those boxes into the house. She couldn't wait to start unpacking and make this place hers.

It didn't take long to settle into a routine at school. Each day remained relatively predictable. Cassie had Danelle, and the comfort of having a good friend took away the unease she had at other new activities.

By the end of the weekend, the Jones were mostly settled in their new home. Mr. Jones surprised the family with a dog and cat from the local animal shelter to christen the house. The kids were delighted and named the cat Baby Blue, because she was a

Siamese with big blue eyes. The dog they named Pioneer. Cassie wasn't sure her mother was as delighted.

This Tuesday Cassie was especially excited, because it would be her first Girl's Club meeting. She'd been a part of the same unit for four years in Texas. One of the first things her mom had done was sign her up here.

Ms. Dawson handed out little blue books to everyone. Cassie opened hers up. It only had one page inside: a white sheet with twenty blank squares centered around an ice-cream cone.

"What is this?" Emmett Schrimmer asked.

"This is your reading log," she said, stepping to the front of the class and smiling at everyone. "When you finish reading a book, you come and tell me, and

I'll give you a sticker. Put it in one of the squares. It has to be a chapter book, not a picture book. Once you have all your squares filled in, I'll take you out for an ice-cream cone."

This announcement was met by cheers and excited chatter from the students. Cassie grinned. Twenty books. She could get that done in a month.

⚪︎〰️✻〰️⚪︎

"Clear your desks and put your books away," Ms. Dawson said. "Then everyone line up."

Cassie glanced at the time. Morning recess. She got in line behind Riley, the blond who never said a word to her. Cassie turned around and smiled at Danelle, who winked at her.

"Let's go!" Ms. Dawson said.

Cassie started after Riley and nearly tripped.

Glancing down, she saw her shoelace was untied. She stepped out of line to tie it, pausing to tighten up the other one, too.

The class continued without her. When she looked up, everyone had gone, including Ms. Dawson.

Cassandra jumped to her feet, anxious to catch up with her class before anyone noticed she was missing. She knew her way to the play yard, at least. She headed that direction, folding her arms in the hall so no one would question why she was out by herself. She marched so that her ponytail swung like a pendulum. Her shadow on the walls entertained her until she got outside.

The first place she headed was the swings. Cassie let herself ride higher and higher into the wind, enjoying the exhilarating feel of freedom that accompanied her. In a moment, she knew Danelle would notice her and come and join her. Until then, she'd just pump as hard as she could. Her eyes swept the play yard, trying to locate her friend with the shoulder-length brown hair. She didn't spot her. She slowed her swinging a bit as she turned to search the soccer field, just in case Danelle had decided to play.

For that matter, she didn't see anyone she recognized.

Cassie's momentum stopped as a feeling of trepidation crept through her chest. She hopped off the swings and ran over to the monkey bars. She climbed along with the other kids, feigning calmness, all the while looking for a familiar face, another classmate. She jumped down and made her way to the other side of the play yard, checking the younger grades' playground just in case.

Her class wasn't here. Cassie was sure of it now.

Maybe they'd gone back to the room. Maybe Ms. Dawson decided to do indoor recess today just for a change.

No one objected when she hurried back into the building. Her heart pounded in her throat, and she could just imagine the trouble she'd be in for losing her class.

The classroom door was open, and she took a deep breath before stepping inside.

No one. The room was empty.

Cassie stood there, blinking back tears. Now what? She was all alone and had no idea where to go.

CHAPTER THREE

Club Girls

It was time to ask for help. Cassie knew where to ask, but the very thought made her knees weak. She needed to walk into Ms. Wade's class and tell her she was lost. Ms. Wade would fix this. But first, Cassie needed to gather all of her courage. She wiped her eyes and prepped herself with several deep breaths.

Then she walked across the hall.

The door was closed, and she hesitated. Should she knock? Or just walk in? She opted for a brief knock before pushing the door open.

Ms. Wade turned from the blackboard and looked at her expectantly. "Yes?"

Cassie focused on the teacher, ignoring the curious staring eyes that latched onto her. She walked over and whispered, "I've lost my class."

Ms. Wade blinked, her expression bewildered, and then in melted into what Cassie hoped was sympathy. "Come on. I'll help you find them." She looked at her students. "I'll be gone for a few minutes. Work on your reading assignment. Monica, take names. If anyone talks or makes noises, let me know."

"Ms. Dawson's your teacher?" Ms. Wade asked as

she led Cassie from the room.

Cassie nodded. "We always have recess right now. But I went out there and no one's there."

"Hmm," was Ms. Wade's non-committal reply. She didn't say anything else as they trooped through the school. "Wait here," she said, stopping outside a room.

Ms. Wade disappeared inside, and Cassie waited. She read the plaque next to the door. "Teacher's Lounge." So this was a room just for teachers. Was Ms. Dawson here? Where was her class, then?

Ms. Wade emerged with Ms. Dawson, who looked Cassie over with bewilderment.

"I'll be going now," Ms. Wade said with a wave.

"Thank you," Ms. Dawson replied, and then focused on Cassie, staring down the bridge of her nose at her. "Why aren't you with the class?"

Cassie swallowed and blinked quickly to discourage the gathering tears. "I stopped to tie my shoe. When I looked up, everyone was gone. I thought they went to recess, so I went too. But no one was there." The treacherous tears were forming in her eyes, in spite of Cassie's best efforts. Suddenly she longed for her old school. She longed for the familiarity of the routine, the hallways, the teachers she knew, the classmates she'd grown up with for years. This school wasn't her place.

Ms. Dawson put a hand on her shoulder. "It's all right. The class is at P.E. We have morning recess every day during the first week of school. After that, we only have it on Mondays. The rest of the week, it's P.E."

"Oh," Cassie said dumbly. What an idiot she'd been to assume she knew the schedule around here. "Where's P.E.?"

"In the cafeteria. Come on, I'll walk you there."

Cassie would rather not go. She didn't want to show up for a class fifteen minutes late and have everyone wonder what happened to her. But she certainly couldn't tell Ms. Dawson no. She trudged along behind, no longer excited about anything this day had to offer.

Cassie walked into the cafeteria timidly. She didn't expect anyone except Danelle to notice she was missing, but several of her classmates spotted her.

"Where did you go?" Karla asked. "You just vanished."

"Cassie!" Danelle gave her a hug. "Did you get sick?"

"I got lost," Cassie said, going for the humble pie. "I thought you guys were at recess."

That earned some polite titters from her classmates, but nobody was rude. In fact, everyone was super nice about it, as if they understood how traumatizing that was for the new girl.

Maybe it's not so bad here, she thought. *Maybe I need to give it more time.*

"Remember, Cassie, you're not a bus rider today," Ms. Dawson said that afternoon as Cassie put her homework in her backpack. "Your mom sent a note. You've got Girl's Club after school."

"Thank you, Ms. Dawson," Cassie said. She hadn't forgotten, of course. How could she? Her stomach was in knots again at the thought of meeting her new unit. She'd been a part of her old troop for four years, starting in Kindergarten. She had been closer to those girls than anyone else at school besides Tammy. Had this unit been together just as long? She'd be the odd girl, the intruder.

The final bell rang. Cassie put on her backpack and picked up her lunch box before making her way to the cafeteria.

She spotted the group immediately. A lunch table was still out, three girls and two women seated around it. Cassie approached but didn't sit down, waiting for someone to speak to her.

One of the women looked up. She was smaller with short brown hair and a round, friendly face. She smiled at Cassie. "Hi, I'm Margaret. I'm your leader.

You must be. . . ?" Her question trailed off in expectation.

Cassie put on a brave smile. "I'm Cassandra Jones."

One of the girls turned around. The one with short blond hair and a face very similar to Margaret's. Riley. "Oh, I know her," Riley said. "She's in my class."

"Well, great!" Margaret stood up and took Cassie's arm, guiding her to the table. "We're so excited to have you. And how nice that you and Riley are already friends!"

Riley hadn't spoken more than three words to Cassie since school started. But now she scooted over to make room. "You can sit by me." She pointed out the other girls. "That's Ciera, Leigh Ann, and Jaiden.

My mom's our leader, but Trisha—" she pointed to the other woman, a taller woman with broad shoulders and wavy red hair. "She's the assistant leader. She's Jaiden's mom."

Trisha didn't smile at the mention of her name. She glanced up and stared at Cassie as if trying to figure out why she was there.

Cassie waited until Trisha looked down, then she whispered to Riley, "I don't think she likes me."

Riley shrugged. "She's moody."

Cassie nodded and shrugged it off as well. She tried to place all the names and faces together, keep them straight in her mind. "We're small."

"There'll be more," Margaret said, handing Cassandra a book.

Sure enough, more girls filed in. Mareen,

Cheyenne, Stacy, Kei, Janice. Still a small group, but not as bad as she'd feared. Her last troop had had about fifteen girls in it.

Margaret led them in a song and a game, and then they worked on their first merit badge: what to do in an emergency. They finished up with another game, then held hands and sang a song about friendship.

Riley didn't let go of Cassie's hand when they finished. She gave it a squeeze. "We're friends forever now."

"Yeah?" Cassie said, caught off guard but also hopeful. She could use another friend. She saw her mom's van pull up outside and gathered up her things. "Bye," she called, running toward the exit.

"Bye," the girls chorused back.

"See you tomorrow!" Riley said, waving.

Cassie let herself into the passenger side and plopped down with a sigh.

"How was it?" her mom asked, giving her a worried look.

"Great!" Cassie said, smiling. "It was great. I made lots of new friends."

CHAPTER FOUR

Blow Up

The week seemed to drag by. Cassie could hardly wait for Girl's Club again. Leigh Ann, Riley, and Cheyenne were in her class at school, and all three girls remained friendly with Cassie. Especially Riley.

Cassie and Danelle were heading for the swings at recess when Riley stepped over.

"We're playing freeze tag by the dome," she said. "Want to play with us?"

Freeze tag! Cassie loved the game. And she hadn't played it since they moved. "Sure! We'd love to." She looked at Danelle for confirmation, but Danelle wore a frown on her face.

"No, I don't think so," she said. "We like to swing."

"You could do both," Riley said, weaving her fingers together in front of her. "Play freeze tag and then swing."

Cassie watched Danelle's expression, but it didn't relent. "We'll swing first," Cassie told Riley. "Then we'll come join you."

"Sure," Riley said. She turned and walked away.

"You don't like freeze tag?" Cassie asked, trying

to feel out why Danelle had reacted that way.

She grunted. "I don't like Riley."

"Really?" Cassie tried to think what Riley could have done to merit such a response. Sure, she hadn't said much to Cassie in the first week of school, but no one had. Riley was shy, just like Cassie was.

Danelle rolled her eyes. "She's so immature."

Cassie considered that statement as they swung higher and higher into the air. Riley was small for her age, but other than her size, Cassie hadn't noticed anything lacking in her behavior. "Did you guys used to be friends?"

"No, but we've known each other for forever. Trust me on this one."

Cassie couldn't stop thinking about Danelle's words all day. They never did join Riley's group for freeze tag, and Cassie felt bad about that. Only when school was out and Riley got up to head for the cafeteria did Cassie jump up and run after her.

"Riley!" she called.

Riley paused and waited, one eyebrow raised.

"Sorry we didn't join you at recess," Cassie said, catching her breath. "We decided to swing the whole time."

"Yeah," Riley said, nodding.

They walked side by side in silence before Cassie ventured, "So do you and Danelle know each other?"

"Not really. We were in the same preschool, but that was like, forever ago."

Wow, Cassie thought. They'd lived around each other that long? Once again, she felt like the odd one out. But how could Danelle possibly know what Riley was like if they hadn't hung out since preschool?

They reached the cafeteria and joined the other girls around a table. Riley's mom came over and talked to her a bit, then joined Trisha at the front.

"Today we're going to make stuffed animals," Trisha said, holding up a bear covered in plaid fabric. Next to her, Margaret smiled down at the girls, expressing all the enthusiasm that Trisha wasn't. "It's really very easy." She went on to demonstrate, and Cassie wished she could freeze-frame the instructions. She could tell already this would be confusing.

"So everyone, pick your fabric and I'll walk you through the instructions again."

Cassie leaned in with the rest of the girls, sifting through the pre-cut fabric shapes and choosing one she liked. "How is this going to be a stuffed animal?"

she whispered to Ciera.

"Cassandra," Trisha said loudly, "I don't need anyone talking while I'm instructing. Please pay attention."

Cassie looked down, her cheeks warming under the chastisement. She tried to pay attention, but her ears buzzed with humiliation.

Everyone was working now, pulling a needle and thread along the edges of their fabric. Trisha was still explaining, but Cassie had missed the first directions. She turned to Margaret, their leader. "I didn't quite get it. Can you show me?"

"Cassandra!" Trisha barked. "Around these parts, young lady, we show respect. If I'm talking, you're not. I don't know if you think you're something special or better than us, but if I have to tell you again to be quiet, you'll spend the rest of the time in your own special corner. Do you hear me?"

Cassie didn't even know how to respond. Her breath came in shaky little gasps, and she thought her eyes would pop out of her head. How could she talk to her that way? What right did she have?

"Answer me!"

All the girls were staring at Cassie, their faces reflecting the shock Cassie felt. She bobbed her head.

"Say, yes, Ma'am. That's how we talk in these parts."

"Yes, Ma'am," Cassie whispered. She fisted her hands together as tremors of anger swept through her. She bit her lip so hard she tasted blood. She wanted to call her mom. Now. She wanted to go home. She couldn't bear to be in the room with this ogre of a woman for one more minute.

Apparently satisfied that Cassie was subdued, Trisha went back to her instructions. Cassie put her piece of fabric down on the table. Without asking permission, she stood up and walked out of the cafeteria. She kept going until she got to the bathroom in the connecting hallway. Only once inside did she allow herself to release the tension she felt.

"How dare she!" she raged at her reflection. Her own wretched face stared back, tears rolling down her cheeks, her brown eyes bloodshot. "Who does she think she is? I was just asking for help! That witch!" She stuck her knuckle in her mouth and sobbed, but the anger was just getting going. She pulled her hand out and hit the mirror, screaming. "I hate her! I hate her! She's so mean, she's so awful! I hate this place, I hate her so much!"

A face appeared in the mirror behind Cassie. She met the eyes of Jaiden, Trisha's daughter. Jaiden turned around and went for the bathroom door.

"Wait, Jaiden!" Cassie cried out, panicking. She reached for Jaiden, anxious to draw her back, but Jaiden didn't wait. She went out, the door swooshing behind her.

Cassie gasped and wrapped her arms around her shoulders. She sobbed, rocking herself back and forth. She knew what Jaiden was doing. At this moment, she was tattling on Cassie, telling Trisha everything Cassie had said in the bathroom. If only she could flee. She should, she should run from here, leave the school. Never come back. She never wanted to talk to Trisha again. She couldn't stay in this group.

The door banged open, hard enough to hit the wall behind it. Cassie dropped her hands to her sides and braced herself. Trisha came in and faced her, lips pursed together and her arms folded.

"What's your problem?" she demanded.

All of Cassie's gusto left her. She tried to be brave. She did not want to cry in front of this woman. "Nothing," she whispered.

"I gave you very basic instructions. All you have to do is follow them. And whatever you think of me, whatever your problem is, you have absolutely no right to come in here and badmouth me."

Cassie blinked, her eyelids feeling swollen and tight over her eyes. She couldn't reason with a madwoman.

"Now I expect an apology from you. Then you

get yourself out of this bathroom and join us. With a good, respectful attitude."

"Sorry," Cassie murmured. She wasn't sorry, not in the least, but she was smart enough to know the only way she'd get out of this was by saying it.

Trisha grabbed the door and yanked it open. "Now go. And I better not hear you talking about this to anyone."

Cassie walked in front, clenching her teeth together.

CHAPTER FIVE

Recoop and Recovery

The girls were stitching up their bears, all of them looking more or less like Trisha's. Cassie shoved aside her piece of fabric and sat down at the table. She slumped over, putting her chin on her fist.

Margaret sat down across from her and picked up the fabric. "Can I help you with this?"

Cassie shrugged. She watched as Margaret put

the bear together, but Cassie didn't offer to help.

"Did she get you in trouble?" Margaret

whispered.

Cassie's eyes burned again, and she closed them. She swallowed hard. *I just want to go home. This will all be over soon.*

A cool hand closed over hers, and Cassie opened her eyes to see Margaret staring at her, sympathy on her face. "I'm sorry."

Cassie nodded and looked away. A small part of her recognized that Margaret was an ally, but the bigger part of her felt betrayed. Margaret was the leader, not Trisha. She could have stood up to her, defended Cassie. Even now she could, tell Trisha she was in the wrong and Cassie hadn't done anything to deserve such treatment.

But Cassie understood that Margaret wouldn't do that. Couldn't do that. She was too timid, and perhaps just as afraid of Trisha as Cassie was.

Cassie didn't speak to anyone the rest of the time at Girl's Club. Everyone finished up with their bears and started a game. Cassie fiddled with her bear, pretending to be too engaged in the project to play. She joined in the closing song only because Trisha called her out, and she'd rather stand there and lip sync than cause another scene.

Then it was finally over, and her mom's blue van pulled around to the side. Cassie grabbed her bag and dashed out.

"What's wrong?" her mom asked as soon as she opened the car door.

Cassie passed a hand over her eyes, knowing it must be obvious that she'd been bawling. Even now she felt the sting, the threat of more tears just below the surface. Her younger brother and sisters argued loudly in the backseat, and she let the noise invade her senses, dull the sharpness of the incident. She took a careful breath. "I don't want to be in this Girl's Club anymore."

Her mom raised both eyebrows. "Really? But you've been so excited all week."

Someone tapped on Cassie's window, and she turned to see Margaret there. Her mom pressed a button, and the window rolled down.

"Hi, Karen," Margaret said, giving a little wave. "I just wanted to talk to you about what happened today."

Cassie shrank back in her seat and avoided eye contact, wishing she didn't have to be here to overhear the conversation.

"What happened?" her mom asked, and Cassie detected a low note of warning in her voice.

Margaret hesitated, her eyes flitting to Cassie. "I didn't see all of it. But Trisha, the assistant leader, got on to Cassie rather harshly. Then Cassie went to the bathroom, and Trisha followed her. I'm not sure what happened then, but I think they had an altercation."

Her mom turned to her, danger flashing in her dark eyes. "She followed you to the bathroom?"

Cassie forced herself to nod. The prickling got to be too much, and the tears managed to work their way down her face.

Her mom turned her attention back to Margaret. "Thank you for telling me. It's Margaret, right?"

Margaret smiled. "Yes. Cassie's a great addition to our unit. My daughter Riley really likes her."

"Thanks again. We'll talk later." Her mom rolled up the window, signaling the end of the conversation. She pulled the car away from the curb. "Cassie, what happened?"

"I don't really know," Cassie mumbled. "She just started yelling at me in front of everyone. So I went to the bathroom. Then she came in and yelled at me some more and made me come out."

Her mom kept her eyes on the road, but Cassie saw the way they narrowed. "That doesn't make sense, Cassie. Why would she just yell at you?"

Cassie exhaled. "She doesn't like me. I was talking to Margaret and she got mad about it. So I went to the bathroom to cry and yell and just vent, you know? But Jaiden followed me in, and Jaiden told on me." She shrugged. "So that's what happened."

"And you don't want to go anymore?" her mom said in a softer tone.

Cassie shook her head. "No. I'm done with that group."

"Well, I won't make you go." She turned down the road that led out of the city and into the country. "We can look for another unit, maybe at a different school. But before we do, I want you to sleep on this and think really hard. It sounds like there are a lot of positives to this group. You have one leader who's really nice and likes you. You have friends. If you can deal with Trisha, you might be able to turn this negative experience around and still have a good time with these girls."

Cassie considered her mother's words. "I'll think about it." Right now, her feelings were so clear. She just wanted out of that group.

～～～✦～～～

Cassie didn't feel much better in the morning. She found a seat by herself on the bus and spent the ride drafting a note to Ms. Buckley, the school counselor. She wrote down everything that had happened. Fresh tears came to her eyes as she rewrote it, and her chin trembled with fury and indignation. No one had ever spoken that way to her before.

And truthfully, she regretted what she'd said, too. She'd been so angry, lashing out verbally and saying things she'd never say in person. Her shame made her feel black and dirty inside.

She finished her note before the bus arrived. She paused by Ms. Buckley's office and found the little mailbox for students to drop notes in. She shoved it inside and crossed her fingers. *Let Ms. Buckley find it soon*, she prayed.

She spent the rest of the day waiting. Her feelings were near the surface, and anytime anyone spoke to her, she found herself close to tears again. She kept glancing toward the door, hoping Ms. Buckley or one of her student helpers would appear.

At recess she told Danelle she wasn't feeling well. She didn't want to swing today. Instead she sat on the sidewalk and played with the grass, tearing up little pieces and searching for four leaf clovers.

Two shoes appeared next to her, and then Riley plunked down on the sidewalk. "Are you okay?" she asked.

Cassie nodded. She rested her chin on her knees and didn't meet Riley's eyes.

"Trisha's mean," Riley continued. "She always has been. I don't know why. Maybe she just doesn't know what to do around kids."

"Does she have any?" Cassie asked.

"A little boy. He's like three or something."

"She shouldn't be a leader, then."

Riley shrugged. "No one else volunteered. My mom couldn't do it by herself."

Cassie supposed that was true, but she still didn't like it. "I'm going to switch groups."

"Really?" Riley fell silent. They both picked at the grass for a bit, adding the pieces they picked to a growing pile on the sidewalk. "Well, that's too bad."

Ms. Dawson blew her whistle. Students stopped their play and began to gather in from the corners of the yard.

"You should come over and spend the night," Riley said.

The invitation caught her off guard. She had a best friend, but so far Danelle hadn't invited her over. She'd expected that to be her first invite. But she quickly brushed it off. "That would be fun."

"Maybe this Friday?" Riley suggested.

"Okay," Cassie said. She felt a little bit of light crack through the blackness in her soul, breaking off a chunk of the dark. "I'll ask my mom."

⚬⟋⟍⟋⟍⚬

It wasn't until two days later that Ms. Buckley appeared in the classroom door. She waved at Ms. Dawson and then looked at Cassie.

"Cassandra," she said, beckoning to her.

Cassie put her pencils back in their box and

shoved her work inside the desk. She stood up and followed Ms. Buckley down the hall, hands clasped in front of her.

They entered Ms. Buckley's office. As soon as the door was shut, Ms. Buckley turned to her, her short reddish-brown bob brushing the tops of her shoulders.

"I'm so sorry I didn't come for you sooner. I've been out of the office, and when I finally found your note, I realized how urgent it was. I could tell how distraught you were. How are you now?"

"I'm okay," Cassie said. "I'm doing a lot better, actually. It was really, really awful. But I'm okay."

"Would you like to talk about it?"

Cassie hesitated. "Well, I just don't know what to do about Trisha. I think she's an awful person. I was thinking about changing Girl's Club groups so I wouldn't have to see her anymore."

"Are you afraid of her?" Ms. Buckley asked, her eyes gentle.

"A little," Cassie admitted. "I don't want her to yell at me again. And I didn't even really do anything."

"So let's talk about how you can cope when someone overreacts. There's not much you can do to stop them. But you can control your feelings. How did you feel?"

"Angry," Cassie said. "I got too angry. I wanted to hurt something."

"That's normal, Cassandra. But you have to learn how to contain that. Or wait until the appropriate moment to vent it."

"Yeah," Cassie said. "I agree with that."

"Do you like Girl's Club?"

"Yes," she said without hesitation. "I love it. I've been doing it since I was five."

"Is Trisha so important to your life that you'd let her take away something you love?"

"No. But I can join a different unit and still be in Girl's Club."

"What about the friends you have here?"

Cassie thought of Riley. "I'll miss them."

"Is it worth it, Cassie? Or can you put Trisha into a small part of your mind as someone who's not important to you? And then shrug it off anytime she's mean to you?"

Cassie considered that. Could she? Was she strong enough to not let Trisha get under her skin? "I could try," she said slowly. "I guess I could give it another week, at least."

Ms. Buckley smiled at her. "I think you're a very brave girl." She turned around to her game shelf. "Now. Why don't we play a game before you go back?"

CHAPTER SIX

Sleepover

"Are you sure about this?" Mrs. Jones asked as she helped Cassie roll up the sleeping bag.

"Yes!" Cassie could hardly wait. Her first overnight since the move. She checked her duffel bag to make sure she had everything she needed. "Let's go! Riley said I could come over anytime after school."

"Patience!" Her mom laughed. "I already spoke to Margaret. I know what time to take you. You need to make sure your chores are done first. Nobody wants to do them for you while you're off having fun."

Cassie uttered a groan but dropped her bag and headed for the kitchen. She unloaded the dishes as quickly as she could, stacking them into neat piles in the cupboards. The trash wasn't full, so she left it alone.

"Okay," she said, skipping into the laundry room where her mom sorted clothing. "I'm ready now!"

"I'm almost done with dinner," Mrs. Jones said. "Ask your dad to take you."

"Dad!" Cassie raced toward the bedroom and plowed into her father as he came into the kitchen. "Mom said to tell you to take me to Riley's house."

He raised his eyes toward her mother. "Does Cassie know how to get there?"

"How would she know that? She's never been there." Mrs. Jones retreated to the dining room and came back with a sheet of paper. "Here's the directions."

He stuck them in his pocket. "Ready to go, kiddo?"

"Yes!" Cassie rocked back and forth on her heels with anticipation. Her first sleepover in Arkansas.

They piled into the car and headed back into town. The road changed from gravel to asphalt as they passed cookie-cutter houses and trailer parks.

Her father finally turned into a large multi-plex apartment, similar to the one they had lived in before moving into their big house.

"Is this it?"

Cassie searched the parking lot for some identifying feature. One apartment had several potting plants overflowing on the ledge. "There!" She spotted Riley coming out the front door with two dogs in tow. "Yes, this is it!"

Her dad pulled up the rest of the way and parked in front of the apartment.

"Hi!" Cassie said, jumping out of the car.

"Hi," Riley greeted. She helped Cassie get her stuff inside. A tall man with long reddish hair stood in the kitchen. "Dad, this is Cassie," Riley said. "Her dad's outside."

"Well, I'll go meet him," he said, letting himself out.

"That's my dad, Len," Riley said, showing Cassie her room. It was down the hall and next to the bathroom.

"This is cool," Cassie said. "I like your house. It's cozy."

"The insulation's coming out." Riley kicked at a crack in the wall. "You can sleep on my bed, if you want. Instead of on the floor." She gestured to the sleeping bag.

"Sure!"

A little boy poked his head in and squirted Riley with a water gun. "Howard!" Riley screeched. She grabbed for him, but he'd already fled the house. She sighed and shook her head. "And that's my horrible little brother."

"Yeah." Cassie nodded. "I know that feeling."

"He knows your brother. Scott? I think they're in the same class."

"Oh, I'll ask him." Cassie glanced around the bedroom. She hadn't noticed another room in the house. "So where does Howard sleep?"

"At the end of the hall," Riley said. "With Mom and Dad. There's another room at the other end of the house, but it's a storage room right now."

"Ah." Cassie nodded her understanding.

"Cassie!" her dad called from the front room.

"Yeah?" she called back.

"Call me tomorrow and I'll come get you. Be good."

"I will!" she answered, rolling her eyes while

Riley giggled.

"Are you hungry?" Riley led Cassie out of her bedroom and back into the square kitchen.

Her stomach rumbled in answer. "Yes."

"You like ramen?" Riley opened a cupboard.

"Ramen?" Cassie echoed. "Like, Top Ramen?"

"I don't know." Riley held up a small crinkly package. "This is ramen."

"Yeah, Top Ramen! I love it!"

"Great. We just call it ramen around here." She tossed her the package. "Let's go eat it." She crossed the kitchen and opened the front door.

"Wait, like this?" Cassie followed her out to the parking lot, holding the package, perplexed. "Where are you going to cook it?"

Riley turned around, her green eyes sparkling.

"You've never eaten it raw? Come on. You're going to love this."

Riley's dad was working underneath his big white pick-up truck. He had it parked on the grass next to the parking lot. Riley climbed up on the hood and helped Cassie join her.

"This is how we eat it," she said. She took the package from Cassie and opened it, then broke off a piece of the noodles. "Then you open the flavor pack." She ripped open the small foil packet. "And you just dip it in. See?" She stuck the noodles in the salty powder and pulled it out.

Cassie watched her bite into the powder-covered noodles. "All right, here goes," she said, tearing off her own piece and trying it. Her teeth crunched down on the raw ramen, and she nearly choked

on the strong flavoring. Her eyes watered, and she

laughed. "Yeah, it's good!" She preferred it cooked,

but this wasn't bad.

"Yeah, I eat it this way all the time. Maybe every day."

The two dogs circled around the truck, barking and wagging their tails. Riley threw them a noodle, so so did Cassie.

"Don't feed the dogs," Riley said. "You'll spoil them."

"But you did," Cassie said.

"They're my dogs."

True. Cassie shrugged it off.

"So who's your best friend?" Riley asked.

"Danelle," Cassie said.

"Yeah? That's nice."

"Who's your best friend?" Cassie asked.

"I don't know. You, I guess."

"Me?" Cassie didn't know how she felt about that. Flattered, maybe, that someone else might like her that much. A little guilty, because she didn't consider Riley her best friend.

The dogs barked again, begging for Riley's attention.

"What are their names?" Cassie asked. They had one dog, Pioneer, named because he was the first animal in their new house, and one cat, a Siamese named Baby Blue. Cassie loved animals. She wished they could have a dozen more.

Riley pointed to the dogs. "That one's Itchy because he's always scratching, and that one's Shut it. No reason. And that one's Scaredy, because he always runs away from us. We can never get him to stay close unless we have him on a leash."

Scaredy. Cassie stared at him, the white and black mutt with a curvy tail and skinny little legs. "I want to hold him."

"He won't let you near him."

She had to try. Cassie hopped off the truck and held out her hand. "Here, boy. Come on, come here."

The dog put his ears down and tucked his tail in closer.

"Come on," Cassie begged. She whistled and clicked her tongue. "I won't hurt you."

He took several steps backward. Hoping to surprise him, Cassie dove at him. With a yelp of fear, the dog turned and ran for the open apartment door.

Riley sat on the truck laughing. "I told you."

Cassie climbed back up. "They're so cute! Can I keep one?"

She stopped laughing. "I don't think we can give them away."

"Let's ask your mom. I bet she says yes!" Cassie couldn't take her eyes off of Scaredy. She desperately wanted that dog.

"Tomorrow, Cassie," Riley replied. "She's not home right now, anyway. She's a nurse, and she's working tonight."

"Oh, okay."

Riley hopped off the truck. "Let's watch a movie."

⚓

Riley's dad shut the dogs up in the laundry room for the night, where they howled and scratched and put up such a fuss that Cassie thought for sure someone would come knocking on the door.

But no one did. She must've fallen asleep

watching the movie, because Cassie woke up once in the night to the staticky buzz of the television. She turned it off, used the bathroom, and curled back up on the living room floor next to Riley.

She woke up again when Riley's dad stepped into the house. "Good morning, Mr. Isabel," she said, as politely as she could.

"Morning," he replied in a gruff voice. He glanced at Riley still sleeping on the floor. "Want some breakfast?"

"Sure." Cassie sat down at the card table pushed up against the wall. A moment later, Riley's dad dumped two hot pieces of French toast on a plate and handed them to her with a bottle of syrup. "Thanks!"

Riley woke up and joined her, and Mr. Isabel made her some French toast also.

"Good morning, girls." Margaret came out of the back room, running a brush through her short brown hair. Dark shadows ringed her eyes, and her voice was thick and groggy.

Cassie swallowed and said, "Hi, Margaret."

"Hi, Mom," Riley said. "Can we go for a walk today?"

"Yes, but stay on the sidewalk and don't go across the street. And don't go in any houses. And take the dogs with you."

A younger voice yelled from the back, "Can I go too?"

"And take Howard with you," Margaret added.

Riley sighed. "Please, Mom? Just us?"

"No." Margaret turned the brush on Riley's hair now, tugging her head as she combed. "I have things to do and need him occupied. Here, Cassie." She moved to the couch. "Come sit so I can brush your hair."

Cassie ran her fingers through her long brown hair, but didn't get very far before they got caught. She watched as Margaret cleaned out the brush and put Riley's strawberry blond hair in a jewelery box already stuffed with hair. "Why are you keeping that?"

"For my dad," Riley answered from the table. "Someday when he goes bald, Mom's going to make him a wig."

"Really?" Cassie sat down in front of Margaret. "Put my hair in, too!"

Howard stumbled down the hallway and came to stop in the middle of the kitchen. "I'm hungry," he announced.

"Well, eat fast," Riley said, clearing her plate from the table. "Or we'll leave without you."

They headed outside, but instead of walking through the parking lot to the sidewalk, Riley led Cassie behind the apartment complex and into the wooded ravine. The three dogs paraded behind them, tails wagging and tongues lolling. Cassie kept glancing back and whistling for Scaredy. Every time she did, he'd stop walking and duck down really low.

"Wait up, Riley!" Howard whined behind them, his legs pumping to reach them.

"Hurry, he's catching up!" Riley whispered. She grabbed Cassie's arm and hauled her down into the overgrown bushes.

"I'm coming, I'm coming," Cassie said, sliding

down the leaves and hopping over branches.

He stayed close behind. They reached the bottom of the ravine, then turned around and started back up. Cassie spotted a large white house beside the apartment complex.

"Who's house is that?" she asked.

Riley looked up from the thorn bush she was gingerly extracting from her shirt. "Oh, that's the manager's house. Adrianne lives there."

"Who's Adrianne?"

"My mean neighbor. You're better off not meeting her."

"Mean neighbor?" Cassie widened her eyes. "What's so mean about her?"

"She steals your friends." Riley picked up a stick and broke it in half. "She tells people lies about you and acts all sugary and sweet."

"But your friends don't fall for it, do they?"
Maybe they did. Maybe that's why Riley didn't have a
best friend besides Cassie.

She didn't answer. She led Cassie to the sidewalk,
and they started walking in the direction of Riley's
apartment. The dogs and Howard were close on their
heels. Cassie wanted so badly to hold Scaredy. He just
wouldn't let her get close.

"Tick check!" Margaret said when they came in.

This was new to Cassie. Riley stood still while
Margaret sifted through her hair and then checked
her clothes. "Make sure you look yourself over when
you change," Margaret told her daughter. Then she
turned on Cassie.

"What's tick check?" Cassie asked, following

Riley's example while Margaret lifted sections of her hair.

Margaret chuckled. "That's right, you're not an Arkansan. Ticks are these little bugs that drop on you from the trees or crawl up from the grass. They latch on to your skin and stay there, sucking your blood. Anytime you go outside, you should check for them."

A shudder ran through Cassie, starting at her hips and going to her shoulders. "Sounds horrible!"

"Eh, they're not so bad. Normal. Just check for them."

Both she and Riley were tick-free. Riley plopped down on the couch and turned the TV on. Cassie joined her, though she'd never seen the show before and had no idea what was going on. Her parents were really strict about television. She only got to watch movies. Sometimes a TV show, but everyone had to agree on it, and with four kids, that wasn't likely.

The phone rang, and Margaret answered it. "Hello, this is Margaret. Oh, hi! Adrianne wants her hair braided? Sure, send her right over!"

Cassie glanced at Riley. "Is that the same Adrianne you warned me about?"

"Watch and see," Riley whispered. "She'll be so super nice to you."

She came to the door a few minutes later. Riley pulled Cassie outside.

"We don't need to watch her get her hair done," Riley said. "Boring, anyway."

"What's that?" Cassie pointed to the small yellow automobile in the parking lot. It hadn't been there when they got home from their walk.

"I don't know."

She and Riley approached it. Cassie stayed back in case it sprang to life and tried to run them over.

"Like my go-kart?"

They both turned around as Adrianne stepped down and joined them. She had wire-frame glasses, and her curly brown hair was held back in a neat French braid.

"That's how I got here," Adrianne continued. "I didn't walk. If that's what you thought." She walked right past Riley and gave Cassie a big smile. "Want to ride it?"

"Yeah, sure, can I?" Cassie said. "It looks fun!" And then she remembered Riley. Adrianne hadn't even said hello to her. "Wait, what about Riley?"

"Riley can ride this some other time. She lives

here, right?" Adrianne rolled her eyes behind her glasses. "I'm Adrianne. What's your name?"

"Cassie. I'm Riley's best friend." The words popped out of her mouth unexpectedly, and Cassie couldn't take them back. Her face burned. She felt like a traitor.

CHAPTER SEVEN

Dog Fight

"Best friend?" Adrianne surveyed Riley again. "I guess you can both ride it. Cassie gets to go first."

Cassie climbed inside, her mind spinning. She nodded at Adrianne's instructions and then drove the little car in a small circle before returning it for Riley. While Riley rode around in it, Adrianne stood by

Cassie.

"Do you like Riley's apartment?" she asked.

Cassie glanced behind her. "Sure." It had everything it needed.

"And all the dogs?" Adrianne arched an eyebrow.

Cassie pointed at Scaredy. "That one. I like him the most. But he runs away every time I try to touch him."

"I'll get him." Adrianne was off like a shot. Cassie couldn't help feeling some admiration at the way she crouched down and blocked the dog's every escape route. Finally, she caught him and returned with him in her arms, a triumphant smile on her face.

"What are you doing?" Riley was out of the go-kart, scowling as she approached them.

"She caught the dog for me!" Cassie held her

arms out, breathless as Adrianne turned the trembling creature over to her. He shook in her arms, thin wiry tail wrapped around his little body.

"We can catch him ourselves, Cassie. Put him down."

Cassie ignored Riley's order. She sat down cross-legged in the grass, cooing at Scaredy and stroking his head. "Don't be scared of me," she whispered. "I love you."

Riley leaned against the garage wall. "Bye, Adrianne."

"Just trying be nice. Geez." She got back in her go-kart. "See you around, Cassie."

Cassie gave a little wave.

"See, she's evil," Riley said, shielding her eyes against the sun with one hand and glaring in the direction Adrianne had gone.

"Yeah," Cassie said, but with Scaredy in her lap, she could hardly condemn Adrianne. Finally, she was getting to hold the dog.

Riley turned to her with a big smile. "But you passed! She didn't steal you away from me! Best friends, right?"

Cassie hesitated. "Well, I'm still best friends with Danelle." She could have two best friends, she supposed.

Margaret came out of the house, walking down the steps and coming outside. "You like that dog, Cassie?"

"I love him." Cassie's hands stroked his little shaking head, tried to calm his fast-beating heart.

"Do you want to keep him? I think we have

enough dogs here."

Cassie lifted her head and uttered a gasp.
"Really? Could I?" She wrapped her arms around
him and cuddled him to her chest. Could he really be
hers?

"Well, I've got to ask your mom."

"What?" Riley sputtered. "We're giving him away? Why? He's our dog!"

"The management said we could have one dog, honey," Margaret said, reaching for Riley. "It's time for them to find new homes."

"Can we call my mom?" Cassie asked, unable to contain her excitement.

"Sure. You'll have to put the dog down."

Reluctantly Cassie helped him out of her lap. She started to ask Riley to keep an eye on him, then thought better of it when she saw her face. Tears streaked down, her eyes swollen and red. She had her arms crossed over her chest and her lips pursed together. Cassie rubbed Scaredy's head. "I'll be right back."

This time, at least, she had her phone number

memorized. She called home and crossed her fingers, hoping her mother would be agreeable. "Hi, Mom!" she said excitedly when Mrs. Jones picked up.

"Hi, Cassandra. How are you? Are you ready to come home? Your dad's about to leave to get you."

"No, not yet. But I have a question. The Isabels have a little dog they're trying to find a new home for. He's super sweet, really obedient, and so cute. Can I —"

"No," her mom interrupted before Cassie could even finish asking. "Don't even let that idea get into your head, Cassie. We already have Pioneer and Baby Blue. We're not bringing home any more animals."

"But, Mom, if you just saw him—"

"No, Cassie." Her mom's voice had taken on the stern, no-questions edge. "You can play with him every time you go to Riley's house."

Until some stranger takes him home. But Cassie kept the thought to herself. She knew better than to argue. "Okay," she sighed.

"Get your stuff together, Cassie. Daddy will be there soon."

"Yes, Mom." She hung up the phone and turned around to Margaret. "She said no," Cassie said, and she couldn't stop the disappointed tears that spilled over.

Margaret wrapped her up in a hug, all softness and sweet-smelling. "It's okay. We'll have him for a bit longer still. Go outside and hold him while you can."

Cassie did as she was told, descending the steps and walking into the bright sunshine.

She spotted Riley right away, sitting on a wood

crate and kicking her legs, staring into the distance.

"Hi," Cassandra said as she approached. She glanced around for Scaredy, but didn't spot him out in the open. "Where's Scaredy?"

Riley bobbed a shoulder in response.

Cassie felt a flash of annoyance. "Come on, Riley. You were out here with him. Where'd he go?"

"I put him away."

"You put him away?" Cassie rolled her eyes. "Okay, where is he?"

Riley pointed to a large draining culvert next to the sidewalk. "In the ditch."

Cassie stared at the ominous darkness in the giant pipe. She did not want to go in there. But how else would she get Scaredy back? She squatted at the edge and hesitated. She could make out shapes in there, but nothing for sure.

"I wouldn't go in there," Riley called. She hadn't moved from the crate. "There are snakes and rats."

Cassie swallowed hard. "Scaredy!" she called softly. "Come here, boy!" She added a quiet whistle to the end. Nothing inside the culvert budged. She whirled on Riley, angry. "Why did you put him in there?"

"Because I don't want you to take him home," she replied, as if it were as simple as that.

"Well, for your information, I'm not taking him home! My mom said no! And now I don't even get to hold him until I go!"

Riley shrugged. "So? You're here to play with me, not my dog."

Was she actually jealous? Cassie couldn't believe

it. "I'll just go call Adrianne and ask her to get him for me!"

"Go ahead," Riley shot back. "I'm sure she'd be happy to have a new best friend."

"*You* are not my best friend," Cassie breathed. "You're not even a friend."

Riley jumped off the crate. "Fine. Go get your stuff and don't come back to my house." She stormed off around the back of the house.

Cassie ran inside, stuffing her things in her bag and grabbing her sleeping bag.

"Everything okay?" Margaret asked from the kitchen sink.

Cassie took a deep breath. She wasn't going to complain to Margaret about her daughter. "Yeah. I'm upset about the dog." Which was true. "My dad's on his way."

"We sure enjoyed having you, Cassie. I hope you'll come again."

Not likely. But Cassie only smiled and nodded. She had her manners.

❧

Cassie spent the rest of Saturday fuming over the loss of the dog and Riley's behavior. She was angry at her mom, and barely spoke to her.

"Are they nice people?" she heard her mom ask her dad.

"Seems like it. Met both parents."

Cassie went to the room she shared with Emily. "Mom is so unfair," she said, tossing her overnight bag on the bed. "Riley's mom wanted to give me one of their dogs and Mom wouldn't let me have it."

"Really?" Emily looked up from where she rearranged her American dolls on the bottom bunk. "What kind of dog?"

Cassie lay down next to her and stared up at the top bunk. "I don't know. Small, white and brown. Maybe a beagle." She didn't have any idea, really, but at least she'd heard of that kind of dog.

"Maybe she'll change her mind. Did you have fun with Riley?"

She opened her mouth to say no, then thought better of it. "Yeah, kind of. She was mean about the dog. She didn't want me to have him." But they'd had a nice time, up until then. Cassie felt a prickling of guilt. She shouldn't have left Riley's house without saying goodbye, at least. She considered calling her, but didn't really know what to say.

"Your dress needs to be ironed, Cassie."

Cassie's mom pulled an off-white, pleated dress out of the closet.

"But I don't have time to iron it," Cassie said, taking the dress off the hanger. "Daddy said we have to leave for Church in ten minutes."

"Then wear a different dress." Her mom pressed her fingers to the bridge of her nose, a sign that she was fighting a headache. She was already dressed in a dark blue, floral print dress, her brown hair curled around her shoulders.

"How about this one?" Cassie pulled out a red one with a pinafore and white collar. Sundays were always so stressful, with her dad yelling and her mom trying to get everyone out the door in time. She didn't want to make it harder, but she didn't want to iron, either.

"That's fine. And brush your hair."

Cassie put the dress on and ran a brush through the tangles of her long hair. Then she stopped in front of her jewelry box. She loved jewelry, and she hated to let a day go by without picking out something sparkly to wear. She chose her favorite locket, a tiger eye on a thick chain. Then she picked out some clip-on pearl earrings and a pink wire bracelet.

She remembered before she'd gotten her ears pierced, her best friend Tammy bought her a whole sheet of stick-on earrings. Cassie had done her best to keep them sticky, putting them back on the sheet after using them. But inevitably, several would fall off when she wore them, and eventually she only had mismatched pairs.

It didn't matter now, because her ears were pierced, but she smiled at the thought of Tammy buying those for her. Cassie knew she should write her a letter or call her, but every time she thought of it, she was in the middle of something. Like getting ready for church.

"In the car, everyone!" her dad yelled, and Cassie slipped on her black shoes and hurried out the door.

The church building looked much the same as the one they'd attended in Texas. Cassie wandered the halls until she got to the Sunday School classroom in the back. She followed a few other kids her age and closed the door behind her.

The teacher stood at the front, her wavy brown hair hitting her shoulders. "Hi, everyone, I'm your new teacher, Sister Garrett . Since I don't know you,

I'm going to call roll." She picked up a piece of paper and cleared her throat. "Matthew Davis."

"Here."

"Gary Faucet."

"Here."

"Riley Isabel."

"Riley!" Cassie burst out. "I know her. She's in my class at school!"

"She's also in your Sunday School class," the teacher said.

"But I've never seen her," Cassie said. "She's never come here before."

"Well, then." The teacher smiled at Cassie. "Hopefully you can be the right kind of friend to bring her back."

Cassie frowned. She hadn't been that kind of

friend when they were fighting.

Her teacher must've seen her hesitation, because she said, "Just include her, Cassie. Invite her to hang out with you and your friends. Join your activities."

She could do that. Maybe Riley would enjoy hanging out with her and Danelle. Their fight was stupid, after all. She made up her mind to apologize the next time she saw her. Maybe they would all be best friends.

The New Girl

Walker Wildcats Year 1

Episode 2: Club Girls

Available now!

They pulled up to the ice-cream shop, and Cassie followed Ms. Dawson inside.

"What would you like?" Ms. Dawson asked.

It just seemed wrong to tell her teacher to buy something for her. Cassie surveyed the menu behind the counter. "Could I have a vanilla waffle cone, please?"

She sat down at a booth and waited while Ms. Dawson placed the order. What would they talk about? Tomorrow's assignment? Her grades? This just seemed so weird.

"So," Ms. Dawson said, returning with the ice cream, "What do you think of Arkansas so far?"

If she had asked Cassie a few weeks ago, the answer would've been very different. "I like it, I think. It's different than Texas. But I'm making friends. I like the school." And now that they were moved into their new house, everything felt better. "We have a dog and a cat. I want another dog, but my mom won't let me have one."

"One dog can be enough."

Cassie shrugged. "Yeah." Riley had a dog that Cassie just loved, and Riley's family was willing to give it to the Joneses. But Cassie's mom put her foot down on the idea.

Ms. Dawson chatted about Cassie's family and the new house, and then Cassie's ice-cream was gone. They got back in the car and Ms. Dawson turned to Cassie.

"Where do you live, Cassandra?"

Cassie squinted at the road in front of them, not even sure where she was. She tried to visualize the turns her mom made when she picked her up from school once a week. Not that it did much good, because they weren't even at the school. "Go left," she said, because she was pretty sure left was the correct direction.

Ms. Dawson pulled out onto the main road. Seven minutes went by before she ventured, "Am I supposed to turn anywhere, Cassie?"

There were farther out of the city now, with

empty pastures and fields dotting the road beside out-buildings and antique shops. "I'm not sure," Cassie admitted. "This looks familiar. We turn left somewhere in here, but I'm not sure where."

Ms. Dawson gave her a look that Cassie couldn't identify. Exasperation? Frustration? Annoyance? She sank into her seat, willing herself invisible. Great. She'd just managed to ruin things with her teacher.

Ms. Dawson pulled the car over into a gas station. She fished around in her purse until she found a cell phone. "I'll call your mom and get directions."

Cassie nodded but didn't say a word. She figured the less she talked, the less Ms. Dawson would remember being upset with her.

About the Author

Tamara Hart Heiner is a mom, wife, baker, editor, and author. She currently lives in Arkansas with her husband, four children, a cat, a guinea pig, and several fish. She would love to add a macaw and a sugar glider to the family. She's the author of the young adult suspense series *Perilous* (*Perilous, Altercation,* and *Deliverer*) and *Inevitable*. She also wrote the not-for-profit nonfiction book about the Joplin Tornado, *Tornado Warning*.

Connect with Tamara online!
Twitter: *https://twitter.com/tamaraheiner*
Facebook:
https://www.facebook.com/author.tamara.heiner
blog: *http://www.tamarahartheiner/blogspot.com*
website: *http://www.tamarahartheiner.com*
Thank you for reading!